I was so thrilled when Emily Gravett agreed to illustrate the book, and she brought so much to it. Did you know that if you laid all the pages of the night-time journey side by side they would make a complete scene of the landscape that Cave Baby and the woolly mammoth travel through?

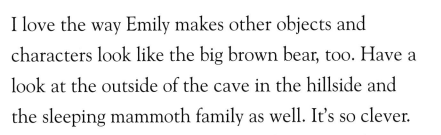

I love the way Emily makes other objects and characters look like the big brown bear, too. Have a look at the outside of the cave in the hillside and the sleeping mammoth family as well. It's so clever.

After I wrote the story, I wrote a Cave Baby song too. My great nieces used to sing it in my live shows, and their little baby sister would be Cave Baby. You can watch a video of me and my husband, Malcolm, performing it on the Gruffalo.com website. Why don't you try singing it too?

And now Cave Baby is ten years old, so not perhaps such a baby any longer! I'd like to wish him, his mum and dad, and all the animals many happy returns indeed.

Julia Donaldson

Cave Baby

Written by
Julia Donaldson

Illustrated by
Emily Gravett

MACMILLAN CHILDREN'S BOOKS

Cave Baby's lucky – he lives inside a cave
With his mum (who's good at painting)
    and his dad (who's very brave)

And a sabre-toothed tiger,
    a hyena and a hare
And a grey woolly mammoth, and a big brown bear.

Cave Baby's lonely. Nobody will play.
Dad is busy being brave. Mum says, "Keep away."

Everything is boring . . .
    Then suddenly it's not,
For in a corner of the cave he finds a brush and pot.

Spots on the hyena!

Stripes on the hare!

Stars on the tiger!

Squiggles on the bear!

Zigzags on the mammoth!

This is lots of fun . . .

But Mum and Dad are furious,
and say, "Look what he's done!"
Cave Mum fetches water. She mutters and she wipes.

No more spots and squiggles!

No more stars and stripes!

Cave Dad wags his finger.

"If you don't take care,
A mammoth's going to throw you to the big brown bear!"

Cave Baby's restless. He's feeling wide awake.
A long grey trunk comes sneaking in,
all wiggly like a snake.

"Where are you taking me?
    Where, tell me where?
Are you going to throw me to the big brown bear?"

Stripes in the forest! A tiger's lurking there. "Don't throw me to the tiger or

the big brown bear!"

Crashing in the bushes! A hare is leaping there. Maybe he's escaping from

the big brown bear!

A cackle in the bracken! A hyena's laughing there.

Has he heard a joke about the big brown bear?

A cave in the hillside! "I wonder who lives there?
I hope it's not . . . Don't let it be . . . the big brown bear!"

The cave is bright with moonlight. The walls are plain and bare.
Snoring in the shadows! Someone's sleeping there.
Cave Baby's worried. He doesn't understand . . .
Until the woolly mammoth pops a paintbrush in his hand.

A five-legged tiger!

A long curly hare!

Horns on a hyena!

A beard on a bear!

A moustache on a mammoth!

This is lots of fun!

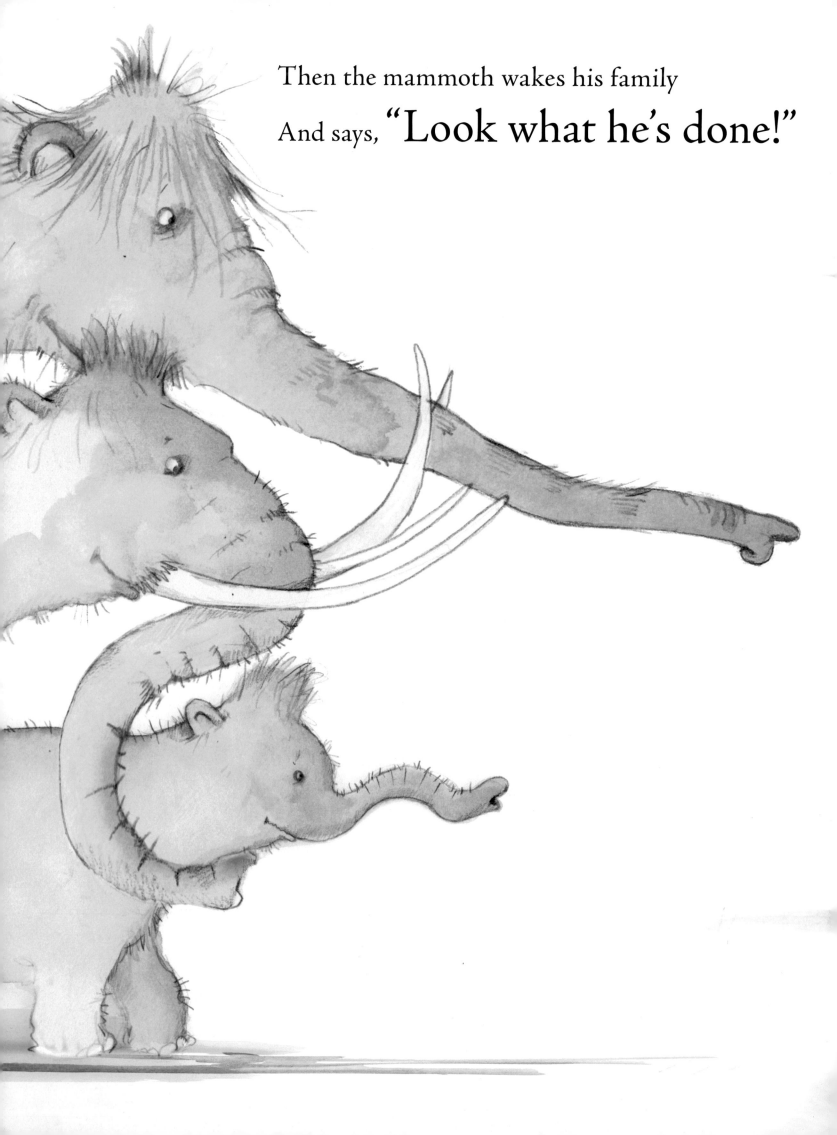

Then the mammoth wakes his family
And says, "Look what he's done!"

And they rollick and they frolic, they trumpet and they crash,
They wade into the water. They roll and romp and splash.

They shake the baby by the hand, then lift their trunks and wave
As the mammoth picks him up again and takes him to his cave.

Cave Baby's happy. He's fast asleep in bed.

He dreams about a tiger with stripes of pink and red,

And a grass-green hyena, and a sky-blue hare,

And a moon-yellow mammoth . . . and a small brown bear.

For Esther Gabriela – J.D.

For Dad & V.W. – E.G.

First published 2010 by Macmillan Children's Books
This edition published 2020 by Macmillan Children's Books
an imprint of Pan Macmillan
The Smithson, 6 Briset Street, London EC1M 5NR
Associated companies throughout the world.
www.panmacmillan.com

ISBN: 978-1-5290-2777-8

Illustrator Emily Gravett drew lots of versions of Cave Baby to make sure he was exactly right. Babies can be quite tricky to draw – little changes can make a big difference to how old the baby looks. It takes a bit of practice to get it perfect! As you can see here, some versions look a little older, and some look a little younger. Emily kept drawing until she had him just right.

He looks a little older here . . .

. . . and a little younger here.

Perfect!

Emily begins by drawing her characters, like Cave Baby, in her sketchbook. She draws them out in pencil first, then adds colour.